1.7

48216 EN
Chickens

Klingel, Cynthia
ATOS BL 1.7
Points: 0.5

LG

Chickens

A Level Two Reader

By Cynthia Klingel and Robert B. Noyed

The Child's World®

2

Chickens make funny sounds. Female chickens are called hens. Hens make a "cluck, cluck" sound.

Baby chickens are called chicks. Chicks make a "cheep, cheep" sound.

5

Male chickens are called roosters. Roosters say "cock-a-doodle-doo."

Chickens are covered with feathers. Chickens have a beak, two legs, two wings, and a tail.

A chicken looks as if it is wearing a red hat. This is called a comb. A chicken also looks as if it has a red beard. This is called a wattle.

There are many different colors of chickens. Chickens can be black, white, red, brown, or orange.

13

Farmers like to raise chickens. Chickens live in buildings called coops. A coop can hold many chickens.

Chickens eat a lot of food. They eat even when they are not hungry. They like corn, oats, and wheat.

Chickens lay eggs. We can buy these eggs for food. Other eggs stay in the nest. Baby chicks hatch from these eggs.

Chickens are funny birds. On the farm we can hear "cluck, cluck," "cheep, cheep," and "cock-a-doodle-doo."

Index

To Find Out More

Books

Coldrey, Jennifer. *The Chicken on the Farm*. Milwaukee, Wis.: Gareth Stevens Pub., 1987.

McDonald, Mary Ann. *Chickens*. Chanhassen, Minn.: The Child's World, 1998.

Potter, Tessa, and Donna Bailey. *Hens*. Austin, Tex.: Steck-Vaughn, 1990.

Web Sites

FeatherSite—Chickens
http://www.cyborganic.net/People/feathersite/Poultry/BRKPoultryPage.html#Chickens
Includes photos, video, and information about various chicken breeds.

Note to Parents and Educators

Welcome to The Wonders of Reading™! These books provide text at three different levels for beginning readers to practice and strengthen their reading skills. Additionally, the use of nonfiction text provides readers the valuable opportunity to *read to learn*, not just to learn to read.

These leveled readers allow children to choose books at their level of reading confidence and performance. Level One books offer beginning readers simple language, word choice, and sentence structure as well as a word list. Level Two books feature slightly more difficult vocabulary, longer sentences, and longer total text. In the back of each Level Two book are an index and a list of books and Web sites for finding out more information. Level Three books continue to extend word choice and length of text. In the back of each Level Three book are a glossary, an index, and a list of books and Web sites for further research.

State and national standards in reading and language arts emphasize using nonfiction at all levels of reading development. The Wonders of Reading™ fill the historical void in nonfiction material for the primary grade readers with the additional benefit of a leveled text.

About the Authors

Cindy Klingel has worked as a high school English teacher and an elementary teacher. She is currently the curriculum director for a Minnesota school district. Writing children's books is another way for her to continue her passion for sharing the written word with children. Cindy Klingel is a frequent visitor to the children's section of bookstores and enjoys spending time with her many friends, family, and two daughters.

Bob Noyed started his career as a newspaper reporter. Since then, he has worked in communications and public relations for more than fourteen years for a Minnesota school district. He enjoys writing books for children and finds that it brings a different feeling of challenge and accomplishment from other writing projects. He is an avid reader who also enjoys music, theater, traveling, and spending time with his wife, son, and daughter.

Published by The Child's World®, Inc.
PO Box 326
Chanhassen, MN 55317-0326
800-599-READ
www.childsworld.com

Photo Credits
© David Woodfall/Tony Stone Images: 13
© Jack Daniels/Tony Stone Images: 2, 6
© James P. Rowan: 9, 18
© Lani/Photri, Inc.: 17
© Martha McBride/Unicorn Stock Photos: cover
© Myrleen Ferguson/PhotoEdit: 5
© Peter Dean/Tony Stone Images: 14
© Photri, Inc.: 10
© Trevor Wood/Tony Stone Images: 21

Project Coordination: Editorial Directions, Inc.
Photo Research: Alice K. Flanagan

Library of Congress Cataloging-in-Publication Data
Klingel, Cynthia Fitterer.
Chickens / by Cynthia Klingel and Robert B. Noyed.
p. cm. — (Wonder books)
Summary: A simple introduction to the physical characteristics and behavior of chickens.
ISBN 1-56766-819-4 (alk. paper)
1. Chickens—Juvenile literature.   [1. Chickens.]
I. Noyed, Robert B.   II. Title.   III. Wonder books (Chanhassen, Minn.)

SF487.5 .K65   2000
636.5—dc21   99-057791